25 Main Street
Newtown, Connecticut 06470

A Cat
and
a Dog

By Claire Masurel
Illustrated by Bob Kolar

A Cheshire Studio Book
NORTH-SOUTH BOOKS / NEW YORK / LONDON

Text copyright © 2001 by Claire Masurel
Illustrations copyright © 2001 by Bob Kolar
All rights reserved. No part of this book may be reproduced or utilized in
any form or by any means, electronic or mechanical, including photocopying,
recording, or any information storage and retrieval system,
without permission in writing from the publisher.

Published in the United States by North-South Books Inc., New York.
Published simultaneously in Great Britain, Canada, Australia, and
New Zealand in 2001 by North-South Books, an imprint of
Nord-Süd Verlag AG, Gossau Zürich, Switzerland.

Library of Congress Cataloging-in-Publication Data is available.
A CIP catalogue record for this book is available from The British Library.

ISBN 1-55858-949-X (trade binding) 10 9 8 7 6 5 4 3 2 1
ISBN 1-55858-950-3 (library binding) 10 9 8 7 6 5 4 3 2 1

For more information about our books, and the authors and artists
who create them, visit our web site: www.northsouth.com
Printed in Italy

A cat and a dog lived in the same house.

But they were *not* friends.

HSSS!

They fought all the time—

and day.

Dirty dog!

They fought about everything—

the best spots,

the best treats.

**But most of all,
they fought about their toys.**

HSSS!

HSSS!

**See these claws?
Stay away from my mouse!**

GRRR!
GRRR!

See these fangs?
Stay away from my ball!

The cat and the dog played on their own.

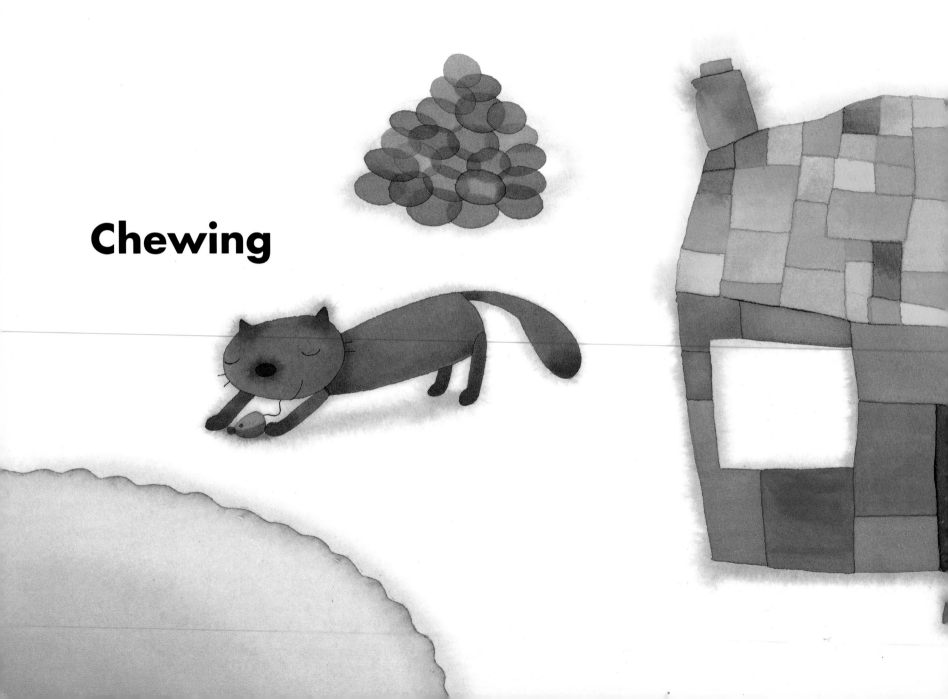

Chewing

Chasing

Rolling

Catching

Then one day,
something terrible happened.

OH, NO!

I can't swim.

**There was absolutely nothing
they could do.**

Nothing?

I can swim!

I can climb!

Here, Cat!

Here, Dog!

A cat and a dog live
in the same house . . .

and now they are the best of friends.